Peppa's Rainbow

Adapted by Em Lune

PEPPA PIG and all related trademarks and characters TM & © 2003 Astley Baker Davies Ltd and/or Entertainment One UK Ltd. HASBRO and all related logos and trademarks TM & © 2022 Hasbro. All rights reserved. Used with Permission.

Peppa Pig created by Mark Baker and Neville Astley.

ISBN 978-1-338-76824-4

10 9 8 7 6 5 4 3 2 1

Printed in the U.S.A.

Licensed by:

22 23 24 25 26

40

First printing 2022

Book design by Salena Mahina

www.peppapig.com

SCHOLASTIC INC.

Peppa and her family are going to the mountains.

"Let's play a game," says Daddy Pig. "We each have to spot a car of our favorite color!"

"Yes!" Peppa and George cheer. This will be fun.

"Let's see which color car comes along first," says Daddy Pig.

Peppa is excited. Her favorite color is red.

Beep beep! Peppa and her family see a green car. "Green is my favorite color," says Daddy Pig. "I win!"

Next, Peppa and her family see Danny and Grandad Dog in an orange tow truck.

"Orange is my favorite color," says Mummy Pig. "I win!"

The next car is blue.

Blue is George's favorite color.

"Yes, George!" says Daddy Pig.
"It's a blue car, so you win!"

Peppa is disappointed. "There isn't a red car anywhere," she says.

Daddy Pig gets an idea. "What color is our car?" he asks.

Peppa thinks about it. "It's . . . red!" she says. "I win! I win!"

Peppa and her family arrive at the top of the mountains. But it's started to rain!

The best thing to eat in rainy weather is . . . ice cream!
Thankfully, Miss Rabbit's ice cream cart isn't far.

"Four ice creams, please!" says Daddy Pig.

He chooses mint, orange, strawberry, and
blueberry flavors.

"Ice cream!" cheers Peppa.

"And look," says Mummy Pig. "They're our favorite colors!"

Mint is green for Daddy Pig, orange is orange for Mummy Pig, strawberry is red for Peppa, and blueberry is blue for George.

Soon, the sun appears, and something else, too—a rainbow!

A rainbow comes out only when it's rainy and sunny at the same time. That is because the light from the sun shines through the water of the rain.

"It's got all our favorite colors in it!" says Mummy Pig.

The colors in the rainbow are red, orange, yellow, green, blue, and purple.

Mummy Pig says that sometimes you find treasure at the end of the rainbow.

"Let's go!" Peppa shouts.

Mummy Pig drives to the edge of a mountain.

But when they arrive, it's stopped raining.
And the rainbow is gone!

"Wah!" George cries.

"Don't worry, George," says Mummy Pig. "Maybe the rainbow has left some treasure behind!"

"There's something over here," Daddy Pig says.

It's a big muddy puddle!

Muddy puddles are made when
the ground gets wet.

"This is the best rainbow treasure ever!" says Peppa.

Peppa loves rainbows! Everyone loves rainbows.

Make-Your-Own Rainbow!

Rainbows are formed when light reflects through water. Water makes the light bend. It is a process also known as **refraction of light.**

Rainbows are pretty. Did you know you can make your own rainbow? Get an adult to help you with this experiment to make your own!

Step 1: Fill a clear glass with water.
Step 2: Place a small mirror in the glass at an angle.
Step 3: Shine a flashlight at the mirror.
Step 4: Look around. (Tip: It might be easier to see if the room you're in is dark!)

You just made your own rainbow!

You can try angling your mirror or flashlight in different ways to see a brighter rainbow. Remember to never shine a flashlight in your eyes (or anybody else's!).

(Note: Sometimes your rainbow might just be a white glimmer. That's still pretty, too! Try again at a different time of day or in a different room for new colors. And of course, when it's raining and sunny, look out a window—you might see a real rainbow in the sky!)